Lizzie Demands a Seat!

Elizabeth Jennings Fights for Streetcar Rights

BETH ANDERSON   Illustrated by **E. B. LEWIS**

CALKINS CREEK
AN IMPRINT OF BOYDS MILLS & KANE
New York

Lizzie Jennings was in a hurry. A big hurry. The kind of hurry she couldn't hold back.

Lizzie's heels ticked off the seconds. If she didn't catch a streetcar right away, the choir would be without an organist. The New York City heat pressed down as Lizzie and her friend Sarah rushed to the corner. At the sight of the horses approaching, Lizzie's hand shot up.

The driver pulled over, and the women boarded.

But the conductor took one look at them and planted himself in the entrance. "You'll have to wait for the next car."

"We can't," said Lizzie. "We're late for church."

He pointed. "There's another car coming. For *your* people."

His words stung. This wasn't about empty seats. It was about tradition—a tradition of separate streetcars for blacks and whites. A tradition most people ignored.

Usually Lizzie's fine clothes and proper manners earned her a seat on a car reserved for whites. Usually it was up to passengers to object.

But not today. *This* conductor expected her to ride on a car for "her people"—a car with the sign "Colored People Allowed in This Car."

Lizzie swallowed hard. "I don't *have* any people."

"The car's full." The conductor shooed her away. "Get off."

She eyed empty seats. Despite being born a "free black" in a "free state," she'd never been treated as equal. She'd been rejected, restricted, and refused by schools, restaurants, and theaters. Suddenly, late-for-church wasn't as important as late-for-equality. Lizzie stood firm.

Passengers murmured.

Horses snorted.

Pedestrians gathered.

Finally, the driver held up the reins. "We need to go."

"Aye," replied the conductor. As he turned to the women, his brogue rolled like thunder. "You may go in. But if the passengers raise any objections, you shall go out . . . or I'll put you out!"

Lizzie's heart pounded. Her voice broke free. "I'm a respectable person, born and raised in this city." She held up a scolding finger. "And *you* are rude to insult a decent person."

"Get out!" The conductor lunged at Sarah and yanked her off the platform. Then he reached for Lizzie.

"Don't you touch me!" she shouted.

He seized her arm.

Lizzie grabbed the window frame and hung on.

He roared at the driver. "Fasten your horses. Give me a hand."

The two men pried her loose, dragged her across the platform, and dropped her at the curb.

But before the driver could snap the horses into action, Lizzie picked herself up and climbed back on the streetcar.

The conductor shook with fury. "You'll be sorry!" He turned to the driver. "Go! And don't stop till you see a police officer."

The whip cracked, the streetcar lurched, and the horses took off.

Lizzie looked back as Sarah faded into the distance.

Five blocks later, the conductor hailed an officer.
Again a crowd gathered and watched in silence.

"Officer," said the conductor, "the passengers object to this woman's presence. It's my duty to remove her."

"No one objected!" Lizzie said, leaping up. "I have rights!"

The officer forced her off the streetcar. "Make your complaint. You'll not get far."

Within moments, the *clippety-clop* of horses' hooves faded and onlookers slipped away. Lizzie stood, catching her breath, while the officer's taunts rang in her ears. She brushed herself off, raised her chin, and straightened her bonnet. Too late and too riled for church, she started home.

Footsteps followed. A voice called out, "Miss?"

Startled, she spun around.

"I saw what happened. Here's my name if you need a witness."

Lizzie studied his card and mumbled, "Thank you."

As she watched him disappear, a flicker of hope sparked. A witness. Someone who recognized her rights!

Slowly she calmed the storm swirling in her mind. This wasn't about her. It was about dignity, about justice—ideas she'd been raised on.

Her enslaved grandfather had fought alongside patriots in the Revolutionary War. Her parents were abolitionists— raising money, giving speeches, fighting to free Southern slaves. Lizzie had joined in the fight for equal rights in the North. She attended meetings. She signed petitions. She became a schoolteacher, determined to educate black children.

But that wasn't enough.

Blacks were shut out of neighborhoods, jobs, and schools.

Nearing home, she glanced at her torn skirt. Clothing could be replaced. Her injuries would heal. Still, injustice remained. Year after year after year.

There was one place where justice for one could mean justice for all.

A courtroom.

But if she failed to win, she could make it worse. Thirteen years before, a black man lost his case for the right to ride. No one had dared try again.

Word of Lizzie's treatment at the hands of the conductor spread through the neighborhood, and a meeting was scheduled for the next day.

At home, stiff and sore, Lizzie recorded every detail of the incident and prepared a statement.

At church, people listened to her words. Elizabeth "Lizzie" Jennings was a respected schoolteacher and church organist. White passengers in the car had not objected. And she had a witness.

The people had waited long enough. They formed a committee and hired a lawyer.

Newspapers printed Lizzie's account.

Her father spoke in churches, wrote letters and articles, and appealed for public support.

Seven months later, in the chill of winter, Lizzie hurried up the walk to the courthouse. The click of her heels matched her heartbeat as she made her way through the crowd.

Stepping into the packed courtroom, Lizzie steeled herself with a silent prayer. She took her seat next to her lawyer, Chester Arthur.

The gavel sounded, and the case began—*Elizabeth Jennings v. The Third Avenue Railroad Company*.

Arthur described Lizzie's attempt to board the streetcar and the assault by the conductor and the driver. He defended her right to ride.

The Third Avenue Railroad Company argued for its right to do what was good for business.

Lizzie weighed every word.

Finally, the judge reminded the jury to keep in mind the facts as they deliberated:

The Third Avenue Railroad Company was responsible for the actions of the driver and the conductor.

People of color had the same right to ride as others.

Streetcars were required to carry all respectable, well-behaved people.

As the jurors filed out, Lizzie studied their faces, one by one. The law seemed clear. But Lizzie understood how words could be twisted. Was it "respectable" to demand her rights? Was it "well-behaved" to fight back? If the jury didn't think so, they could deny her right to ride.

At last the jury returned. The gavel sounded, and a hush settled over the room.

Lizzie's pulse pounded as the judge announced the verdict.

Lizzie turned to her lawyer, then took in the crowd—her family, the committee, her friends and neighbors. They had done it!

The next day, when the "Colored People Allowed in This Car" signs on those Third Avenue streetcars came down, Lizzie smiled. She knew it was just one ruling against one streetcar company, but it was a beginning. More people needed to step up onto streetcars to test the verdict.

And step up they did!

A few days after Lizzie's victory, a woman fought for a seat on an Eighth Avenue streetcar. Then it happened again. And again.

City after city.

Decade after decade.

For a century.

Fighting for the right to ride.

Men and women, young and old, stepped onto streetcars, trains, and buses.

Inspired by the strength of those who came before them.

> ## "Memories of our lives, our works and our deeds will continue in others."
> —*Rosa Parks*

AUTHOR'S NOTE

Elizabeth "Lizzie" Jennings (above) was raised in a New York City neighborhood of free blacks and immigrants. Unlike many African Americans at the time, Lizzie was wealthy and educated. Her parents, involved in the abolitionist movement as well as the fight for equal rights in the North, immersed Lizzie in the struggle for racial equality from an early age. Her father used most of his income from his tailoring business, boarding house, and dry-cleaning patent for the abolitionist cause. The family raised funds to aid escaping slaves and help the poor; they hosted meetings and gave speeches. Lizzie was fortunate that they had both the money and the connections to take her case to court. As leaders in the black community, they knew others involved in the fight for equal rights, such as Frederick Douglass and James W. C. Pennington. They had access to white lawyers who were willing to take on such a case and to newspapers that would publicize their efforts.

When Lizzie boarded the streetcar on July 16, 1854, she was twenty-four years old. Segregation on public transportation in New York City was a custom rather than a law. If white passengers didn't object, black passengers were allowed to ride in the same car. Blacks never knew if they'd get a seat, face violence, or be forced to wait for the crowded, unreliable, dirty cars marked "Colored People Allowed in This Car."

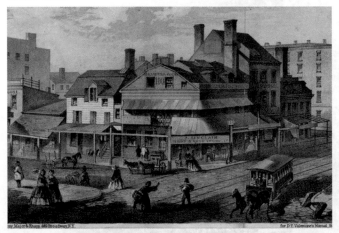

A print of the corner of Pearl and Chatham Streets where Lizzie hailed a horse-drawn trolley.

Jennings v. Third Avenue Railroad Company, February 22, 1855, was the first recorded court case won in the fight for equal rights on public transportation. Unfortunately, there are no court records to provide further details of the proceedings. We cannot verify that the German bookseller who volunteered to be a witness testified in court, and we do not know the composition of the jury. While black men could vote, and therefore could legally have been on a jury, it is unlikely that they were. Again, tradition probably ruled with a jury consisting of white males. Since Lizzie had a financial stake in the outcome of the case, she would not have been allowed to testify. Most of the jury reportedly agreed that the company should pay the requested damages of $500, but some

This photograph of Chester Arthur was taken a few years after he represented Elizabeth Jennings in court.

held out for a lesser amount because of Lizzie's race, and she received $225. Her lawyer, Chester A. Arthur, participated in several civil rights cases and went on to become the twenty-first president of the United States.

Lizzie's case set a movement in motion. Five days after her victory, a black woman was thrown off an Eighth Avenue streetcar. No passengers objected to the woman's presence, but no one spoke up for her either. And so it continued until Lizzie's father joined with others to form the Legal Rights Association. They encouraged peaceful disobedience and helped victims of discrimination take their cases to court. Some cases were won and some lost. Ten years after the Jennings case, the other New York City streetcar companies finally ended the use of separate cars for blacks and whites. Segregation on all public transit in New York City was not outlawed until 1873.

It took many years and many people to change laws in different cities and states throughout the country. On March 2, 1955, a century after Lizzie's verdict, fifteen-year-old Claudette Colvin was arrested for refusing to give her seat to a white person on a bus in Montgomery, Alabama. Nine months later, on December 1, Rosa Parks was arrested for the same act, and her case gained national attention. As in 1854, civil rights leaders organized their efforts and took legal action, but this time they also encouraged all African Americans not to ride the city buses. The Montgomery Bus Boycott, which began on December 5, 1955, caused the bus company to suffer economically. Meanwhile, Claudette Colvin's case was brought to court to challenge the legality of segregation.

The case was appealed to the United States Supreme Court, and on November 13, 1956, the court ruled segregation on buses unconstitutional. The bus boycott ended after 381 days, on December 20, 1956. Finally, one hundred and two years after Lizzie demanded a seat, her battle for African Americans' right to ride freely and equally was won.

Elizabeth Jennings later married Charles Graham and became Elizabeth Jennings Graham. She dedicated her life to educating African American children. In 1895, after teaching in the public schools for many years, she opened the first kindergarten for black children. She operated it until her death in 1901.

In 1991, four sixth-grade girls in New York City learned about Elizabeth Jennings and petitioned their city council to name the corner where she boarded the streetcar in her honor. They were unsuccessful. In 2007, a group of third- and fourth-grade students from Public School 361 in New York City again sought to honor Elizabeth Jennings. After a year of petitioning their city council and attending council meetings, they were successful. The sign for Elizabeth Jennings Place now stands at the New York City bus stop at Spruce and Park Row (originally Chatham Street), a few blocks from the corner where Lizzie hailed the streetcar in 1854.

In 2019, the "She Built NYC" program chose Elizabeth Jennings Graham as one of the first five trailblazing women to be honored with a public monument. Upon completion, you'll find Lizzie near New York City's Grand Central Station.

A NOTE ABOUT THE RESEARCH
The facts related in Lizzie's story are true. The dialogue closely follows her account as it appeared in newspapers of the time. One detail was not included, however. The streetcar to which the conductor pointed—the one bearing a "Colored People Allowed in This Car" sign—pulled alongside while Lizzie and the conductor were engaged in their standoff. The car was full and continued on.

BIBLIOGRAPHY*

PRIMARY SOURCES

"Court Record." *Brooklyn Daily Eagle* [New York], 23 Feb. 1855, vol. 14, no. 46, p. 3. bklyn.newspapers.com. Accessed 22 June 2015.

"For Frederick Douglass' Paper." *Frederick Douglass' Paper* [Rochester, NY], 24 Sep. 1854. Library of Congress.

"From Our New York Correspondent." *Frederick Douglass' Paper* [Rochester, NY], 12 May 1854, vol. 7, issue 21, no. 333. New York Heritage Digital Collections. Accessed 2 Sept. 2015.

"Legal Rights Vindicated." *Frederick Douglass' Paper* [Rochester, NY], 2 Mar. 1855. Library of Congress.

"A New-York Scene." *New-York Daily Tribune*, 27 Feb. 1855, p. 8. Library of Congress, Chronicling America. Accessed 22 June 2015.

"Outrage Upon Colored Persons." *New-York Daily Tribune*, 19 July 1854, p. 7. Library of Congress, Chronicling America. Accessed 18 Jan. 2015.

"The Right of Colored Persons to Ride in the Railway Cars." *Pacific Appeal* [San Francisco], 16 May 1863, vol. 2, no. 7, p. 3. California Digital Newspaper Collection. Accessed 23 Jan. 2015.

"Rights of Colored People Vindicated." *Anti Slavery Bugle* [New-Lisbon, OH], 10 Mar. 1855, vol. 10, no. 30, p. 3. Library of Congress, Chronicling America. Accessed 22 June 2015.

"A Wholesome Verdict." *New-York Daily Tribune*, 23 Feb. 1855, p. 7. Library of Congress, Chronicling America. Accessed 5 Feb. 2015.

OTHER SOURCES

Alexander, Twylla. "The Story of Elizabeth Jennings: Lower Manhattan's Rosa Parks." *Downtown Magazine NYC*, 21 Feb. 2012. Accessed 18 Jan. 2015.

Benson, Kathleen. "A Civil Rights Victory in Old New York." Editorial. *New York Times*, 23 Sept. 1994. Accessed 26 Mar. 2017.

"Elizabeth Jennings." *Elizabeth Jennings*. Columbia University, n.d. Accessed 17 Jan. 2015. projects.ilt.columbia.edu/Seneca/AfAMNYC/Jennings2.html.

"Elizabeth Jennings Graham, Streetcar Rebel." *Figah*. Filling In the Gaps in American History (FIGAH), n.d. Accessed 18 Jan. 2015.

"Elizabeth Jennings, NY's 'Rosa Parks' with Attitude." Blog post. *Narrative Network*, 2 Mar. 2013. Accessed 18 Jan. 2015.

Finkelman, Paul, PhD. "The New York courts in the 1850s." Telephone interview with author, 9 Oct. 2015.

Greider, Katharine. "The Schoolteacher on the Streetcar." *New York Times*, 12 Nov. 2005. Accessed 17 Jan. 2015.

Hewitt, John H., Jr. "Chapter 6: Elizabeth Jennings, A Woman to Remember." *Protest and Progress: New York's First Black Episcopal Church Fights Racism.* New York: Garland, 2000, pp. 97–116.

"Jennings v. Third Ave. Railroad Incident." *African American Registry*. n.d. Accessed 5 Feb. 2015.

Kelley, Blair Murphy. *Right to Ride: Streetcar Boycotts and African American Citizenship in the Era of Plessy v. Ferguson.* Chapel Hill: University of North Carolina Press, 2010. 18–22, Google Books. Accessed 27 Jan. 2015.

Lewis, David. "Graham, Elizabeth Jennings (?–1905)." *The Black Past: Remembered and Reclaimed.* BlackPast.org, n.d. Accessed 17 Jan. 2015.

Mikorenda, Jerry. "New York's First Freedom Rider." Blog post. *The Gotham Center For New York City History*. Graduate Center, City University of New York, 11 Feb. 2015. Accessed 24 July 2016.

*Websites active at time of publication

Reeves, Thomas C. *Gentleman Boss: The Life of Chester Alan Arthur*. New York: Knopf, 1975. 14–15, Google Books. Accessed 24 July 2016.

Robinson, Eric. "Before Rosa Parks: Taking On New York's Segregated Street Car Companies." New-York Historical Society, 18 July 2012. Accessed 12 Dec. 2015.

Smith, James McCune. *The Works of James McCune Smith: Black Intellectual and Abolitionist*. John Stauffer, ed. New York: Oxford University Press, 2006. 98–102. Google Books. Accessed 2 Sept. 2015.

Sterling, Dorothy, ed. *Speak Out in Thunder Tones: Letters and Other Writings by Black Northerners, 1787–1865*. Garden City, NY: Doubleday, 1973.

Virella, Kelly. "7 Heroic Black Women of the 1800s." *Dominion of New York*, 19 Mar. 2012. Accessed 18 Jan. 2015.

Volk, Kyle G. "5 'Jim Crow Conveyances' and the Politics of Integrating the Public." *Moral Minorities and the Making of American Democracy*. New York: Oxford University Press, 2014, pp. 132–66.

"Who Came Before Rosa Parks?" *Beyond Black & White*, 20 Jan. 2013. Accessed 18 Jan. 2015.

SOURCE FOR QUOTATION

"The Meaning of Life: The Big Picture." *Life Magazine*, Dec. 1988, n.p. Accessed 26 Mar. 2017.

FOR FURTHER READING

Freedman, Russell. *Freedom Walkers: The Story of the Montgomery Bus Boycott*. New York: Holiday House, 2006.

Giovanni, Nikki. *Rosa*. New York: Henry Holt, 2005.

Hearth, Amy Hill. *Streetcar to Justice: How Elizabeth Jennings Won the Right to Ride in New York*. New York: Greenwillow Books, 2018.

Hoose, Phillip. *Claudette Colvin: Twice Toward Justice*. New York: Farrar, Straus and Giroux, 2009.

Kittinger, Jo. *Rosa's Bus: The Ride to Civil Rights*. Honesdale, PA: Calkins Creek, 2010.

Parks, Rosa, and Jim Haskins. *Rosa Parks: My Story*. New York: Dial Books, 1992.

ACKNOWLEDGMENTS

Many thanks to all the librarians, historians, and archivists who answered my questions, pointed me to sources, and searched for court records. Special thanks to Paul Finkelman, PhD, president of Gratz College, who helped me understand New York courts in the 1850s. Thanks also to Matt Wall, Chester A. Arthur Presidential Library and Museum, and to Rebecca Haggerty, research archivist at New York Transit Museum.

PICTURE CREDITS

Alamy: 29

Digital Collections, The New York Public Library: 28 (right)

Kansas State Historical Society: 28 (left)

Lonto-Watson Collection, 2010.20.4.31.72; Courtesy of the New York Transit Museum: 31

On July 26, 1917, the Bleecker Street & Fulton Ferry Line, the last horse-drawn streetcar line, stopped running.

To Everett, Paxton, Corinne, and Lillian.
And all who find the courage to stand up for what's right.
—BA

To the countless men and women who fight on the front lines
in the battle for civil rights.
—EBL

NOTE FROM THE ARTIST

I decided to go in a completely different direction when I painted
this book. Normally I use a muted palette, but I wanted to go all out in
the way of color— to stretch my own internal prism. It was very scary,
but as the saying goes, "Nothing ventured, nothing gained." I even had to
purchase colors I never owned or used in my life, such as lavender,
periwinkle, gamboge nova, lilac, manganese blue nova, and opera.
It was a wild and frightening ride but I must say, I truly enjoyed
the journey.

For information about permission to reproduce selections from this book,
please contact permissions@bmkbooks.com.

Calkins Creek
An Imprint of Boyds Mills & Kane
calkinscreekbooks.com
Printed in China

ISBN: 978-1-62979-939-1
Library of Congress Control Number: 2019939439

First edition
10 9 8 7 6 5 4 3 2 1

Design by Barbara Grzeslo
The text is set in Garamond 3.
The illustrations are done in watercolor on hot-press paper.